THE DANCING GIRL
OF GANYMEDE

THE DANCING GIRL OF GANYMEDE

by Leigh Brackett

She had come to life, but she was not human. If Harrah had seen her before he would not have forgotten. He thought that no man could ever forget her.

I: The Wanderer

Tony Harrah came into the bazaar of Komar, heading for the Street of the Gamblers. The sour wine was heavy in him and his pockets were light and he was in no hurry. Win or lose, there was nothing to be in a hurry about. He was on the beach and Komar is a far lost beach for an Earthman.

The wind blew slowly through the narrow streets, stirring the torch flames that burned eternally under the dim red sky. It smelled of heat and sulphur, of the volcanic heart of Ganymede. Even here on the plateau, a thousand feet above the jungle, there was no escape from it. The sliding roofs of the houses were open wide to receive it for there was no other breath of air.

Above the tumult of the bazaar the great yellow star that was the Sun blazed splendidly in the far darkness of space. Jupiter filled half the sky, misty, banded with crimson and purple and grey. Between Sun and Jupiter raced the thronging moons, catching light now from one, now from the other, burning, flashing, glorious.

Harrah took no joy in that magnificence. He had looked at it too long.

He shouldered his way toward the square where the Street of the Gamblers joins the Street of Maidens and the Street of Thieves and at his heels like a furry shadow came Tok the aboriginal, the lemur-eyed child of the forests, who was Harrah's and who loved him utterly.

5

THE DANCING GIRL OF GANYMEDE

It was on the edge of the square that Harrah caught the first wild rhythms of the music. And it was there that Tok reached out one sudden hand-like paw and caught his master's shirt and said, "Lord—wait!"

Harrah turned, startled by the urgency in Tok's voice. He opened his mouth to speak but he did not speak. The look in Tok's eyes stopped him. A queer blank look, luminous with some great fear.

The aboriginal moved forward, past Harrah, and then became a motionless shape of darkness between the torches and the moons. His head was lifted slightly into the wind. His nostrils quivered and gradually the quivering spread over his whole slim body as though he breathed in terror with every breath. Imperceptibly his flesh seemed to shrink in upon itself until all the look of humankind was gone from him and he was an animal poised for flight.

"Lord," he whispered. "Evil, Lord—evil and death. It is in the wind."

Harrah repressed a shiver. He could see nothing but the crowded square—the polyglot life of Komar, the landless, the lawless, the unwanted and forgotten, the mingled off-scourings of the Inner Worlds, mixed with the dark native-human folk of Ganymede. The only unusual thing was the music and there was nothing fearsome in that. Pipe and drum and a double-banked harp, raw and barbaric but stirring to the blood.

Yet Tok half turned and looked at him with the eyes of one who has seen forbidden things and cried out, "Go! Go back, Lord. The wind is full of death!"

And as he spoke others of his kind came running from the square, furry man-things far from their native jungles, and one of them whimpered as he ran, "Demons. Demons with the eyes of darkness!"

"Go, Lord," whispered Tok.

The power of suggestion was so strong that Harrah almost obeyed. Then he caught himself and laughed. "What is it, Tok?" he demanded, in the simple aboriginal speech. "I see no demons."

"They are there. Please, Lord!"

"Nonsense." He jingled the coins in his pocket. "Either I win some money or you steal to feed us. Go back yourself."

He patted Tok's quivering shoulder and went on into the square, forging his way through the crowd. He was curious now. He wanted to see what had frightened Tok and set the aboriginals to flight.

*

He saw the dancing girl, whirling crimson and white across the dirty stones, to the music of pipe and drum and harp, played by three men who might have been her brothers.

She was a Wanderer, from her ornaments and her ragged dress—a sort of interplanetary gypsy, one of the vast worldless tribe of space who travel from planet to planet but are citizens of none. Their blood is a mixture of every race in the System capable of cross-breeding and they are outcaste below the lowest.

There had been a few of them in Komar but this girl was new. If Harrah had seen her before he would not have forgotten. He thought that no man could ever forget her. There was something about her eyes.

Half naked in her bright rags she went on swift white feet through the tossing glare of the torches. Her hair was tawny gold and her face was the face of a smiling angel and her eyes were black.

They did not smile, those dark, deep eyes. They had no kinship with the lithe gaiety of her body. They were sorrowful and smoldering and full of anger—the most bitter raging eyes that Harrah had ever seen.

THE DANCING GIRL OF GANYMEDE

He pushed forward, farther still, until he stood in the open space where she danced, so close that her loose mane of hair almost brushed him as she passed. And as he watched he became aware of an odd thing.

The music was sensuous and the very steps of the dance were an invitation as old as humankind. Yet in some peculiar way the girl took the primitive animal rhythms and transmuted them into something cool and lovely. An old old memory came back to Harrah, of silver birches dancing in the wind.

Then, abruptly, she came to a halt before him, her arms high above her head, poised on a quivering note of longing from the reed pipe. She looked at him, the dark, sinewy Earthman with a handful of coins, and her look was a curse.

He could feel the hatred in her as a personal thing, alive and thirsting. The violence of it shook him. He was about to speak, and then she was gone again, blown like a leaf on the surging music.

He stood where he was, waiting, in the grip of a sudden fascination that he had no wish to break. And between his feet as he watched a small brown cur slunk snarling.

The dogs of Komar are like many another pack on worlds far from their parent Earth. Lost, strayed or abandoned from the ships that land there out of space, they have thriven in the gutters and the steaming alleys. And now, quite suddenly, Harrah became aware of a new sound in the bazaar.

The narrow streets were as full of noise as ever and the wild oblique rhythms of the music filled the square. But the little brown cur lifted his muzzle to the sky and howled, a long savage wail, and somewhere close by another dog-throat picked it up, and another, and still another, until the square rang with it. Harrah heard the cry spreading out and away, running through the twisting alleys and the dark ways of Komar, howl answering howl, desolate and full of fear, and a coldness crept along the Earthman's spine.

There was something terrible about that primitive warning out of Earth's far past, unchanged even on this alien moon.

The music faltered and died. The girl stopped her dancing, her body half bent, poised and still. A silence fell across the square and gradually the sound of human voices ceased entirely as the city listened to the howling of its dogs.

Harrah shivered. The crowd began to stir uneasily and a little muttering began to creep under the wailing of the dogs. The dancing girl relaxed very slowly from her pose, gathering herself.

A rough body brushed Harrah's knee. He looked down to see a great lurcher moving half-crouched into the open space. He realized then that the square was full of dogs, furtive shadows gliding between the legs of the men. They had stopped howling, these dogs. They growled and whimpered and their white fangs gleamed.

The small brown cur moaned once. Then he went with a rush and a scrabble out across the stones and leaped straight for the dancing girl's throat.

II: The Brothers

She did not scream. She moved, as swiftly as the dog, and caught the wiry brown body in mid-leap, between her two hands. Harrah saw her stand so for a split second, holding the frenzied beast that was shrieking now to get at her, and her eyes had narrowed to two slits of cold fire, utterly black and without fear.

Then she threw the dog into the jaws of the lurcher, that had started a rush of his own, and the two went down in a snarling tangle.

After that there was bedlam. The one act of violence was all that was needed. The crowd turned and rolled in upon itself in a panic desire to be quit of the square. Dogs and humans were mixed in a trampling screaming turmoil. Something had set the beasts mad and in their madness they snapped and tore at whatever got in their way. There began to be blood on the stones and weapons flashed in the torchlight and the voice of fury bayed in the hot wind.

Dogs and men only fought there. The aboriginals were gone.

Harrah managed to stand his ground for a moment. He saw the girl run past him and brought the barrel of his gun down across the head of a long-jawed brute that came at her from behind. When he looked again she had disappeared.

The press of the crowd bore him on then, the way she had gone. After a few paces he stumbled and looked down to see scarlet cloth and white flesh between his feet. She was trying to get up. He fought a clear space for her, battering with fists and elbows. In a second she was up, tearing like a wildcat with her long nails at the bodies that threatened to crush her down again.

She was still not afraid.

Harrah grinned. He caught her up and tossed her over his shoulder. She was small, and surprisingly light. He let the tide carry them, concentrating only on keeping his feet, clubbing dog and man alike.

The girl had drawn a little knife from somewhere in her rags. Hanging head down over his shoulder, she plied it and laughed. Harrah thought that it was fine to be brave but he thought she needn't have enjoyed it so much. Her body was like spring steel, clinging around him.

An alley mouth opened before him. He went down it with a rush of escaping humanity and raging dogs, making for the wall. The houses were irregularly built and presently he found a crevice between two of them that had once housed a stall. He dodged into it, set the girl on her feet behind him and stood getting his breath back, watchful of the crowd still streaming by not a foot away from him.

He knew that the girl was looking at him. She was very close in that cramped space. She was not trembling nor even breathing hard.

"Why did you glare at me like that, in the square?" he asked her. "Was it personal or do you just hate all men?"

"Did you pick me up just to get the answer to that question?" She spoke English perfectly, without a trace of an accent, and her voice was as beautiful as her body, very clear and soft.

"Perhaps."

"Very well then. I hate all men. And women too—especially women."

She was matter-of-fact about it. It came to Harrah with a small qualm that she meant it. Every word of it. He was suddenly uneasy about having her little knife where she could use it on his back.

He turned around, catching her wrist. She let him take the knife, smiling a little.

"Fear," she said. "Always fear, no matter where you are."

12

"But you're not afraid."

"No." She glanced past him, into the alley. "The crowd is thinning now. I will go and find my brothers."

A big rusty-red mongrel thrust his head into the crevice and snarled. Harrah kicked him and he slunk back reluctantly, his lips winkled, his red-rimmed eyes fixed on the girl.

"I wouldn't," said Harrah. "The dogs don't seem to like you."

She laughed. "I haven't a scratch on me. Look at yourself."

He looked. He was bleeding in a number of places, and his clothes were in shreds.

He shook his head.

"What the devil got into them?" he demanded.

"Fear," said the girl. "Always fear. I will go now."

She moved to pass him, and he stopped her. "Oh, no. I saved your life, lady. You can't walk away quite so easily."

*

He put his hands on her shoulders. Her flesh was cool and firm, and the strands of her tawny mane curled over it between his fingers. What mingling of alien strains had bred her he could not guess but she was like no one he had ever seen before, inexpressibly lovely in the light of the flashing moons. She was like moonlight herself, the soft gleam of it in her hair, her skin, her great haunted eyes.

Outcaste, dancer in the public streets, pariah in crimson rags, there was a magic about her. It stirred Harrah deeply. Some intuition warned him to take his hands from her and let her go, because she was a stranger beyond his knowing. But he did not. He could not.

He bent and kissed her lightly between the brows. "What's your name, little Wanderer?"

"Marith."

Harrah knew that word, in the lingua franca of the thieves' markets. He smiled.

"And why should you be called 'Forbidden'?"

Her dark gaze dwelt upon him somberly. "I am not for any man to love."

"Will you come home with me, Marith?"

She whispered, "I warn you, Earthman—I am death!"

He laughed and gathered her into his arms. "You're a child and children should not be full of hate. Come home with me, Marith. I'll only kiss you now and then and buy you pretty things and teach you how to laugh."

She did not answer at once. Her face was distant and dreaming as though she listened to some far-off voice. Presently she shrugged and said, "Very well. I will come."

They started off together. The alley was deserted now. There were lingering sounds of turmoil in the bazaar but they were far away. Harrah led the girl toward his house and the streets were empty and still under the thronging moons.

He kept his arm around her. He was full of a strange excitement and his bored ill-temper had left him completely. Yet as he walked he became aware again of a gulf between him and Marith, something he could not understand. A pang of doubt that was almost fear crossed his heart. He did not know what he held, child, woman or some alien, wicked creature, close in the hollow of his arm.

He remembered the aboriginals, who had cried of death and demons. He remembered the howling of the dogs. And he wondered because of what he felt within himself.

But she was very lovely and her little white feet stepped so lightly in the dust beside his and he would not let her go.

They had left the bazaar behind them. They came to a quiet place, surrounded by the blank walls of houses, and suddenly, without sound, as though they had taken form ghost-like from the shadows, two men stepped out and barred their way.

One was an Earthman, a large man, heavy-shouldered, heavy-faced, with a look of ponderous immovability about him. The other was a Venusian, slim and handsome, with bright pale hair. Both men were armed. There was something infinitely ominous about the way they stood there, neither moving nor speaking, with the moonlight touching a hard blue glitter from their guns.

Harrah stopped, his hands half raised, and Marith moved forward, one step, away from him. Then she too stopped, like a crouching cat.

Harrah said, "What is this? What do you want?"

The Earthman answered, "We want the—the girl, not you." His slow, deep voice hesitated oddly over that word, "girl."

Marith turned. She would have fled past Harrah, back the way they had come, but again she came to a dead halt.

"There is someone behind you," she said. Her eyes looked at Harrah and he was startled to see that they were full of terror. She was afraid now—deathly afraid.

"Don't let them take me," she whispered. "Please don't let them take me!" And then, as though to herself, "Hurry. Oh, hurry!"

Her head moved tensely from side to side, the head of an animal seeking escape, but there was no escape.

*

Harrah glanced over his shoulder. A third man had come from somewhere to stand behind them with a gun, a yellow-eyed Martian with a smiling, wolfish face. Deep within Harrah a small chill pulse of warning began to beat. This was no spur-of-the-moment holdup.

15

THE DANCING GIRL OF GANYMEDE

This was ambush, carefully planned. He and Marith had been deliberately followed, herded and trapped.

"Marith," he said. "Do you know these men?"

She nodded. "I know them. Not their names—but I know them." It was terrible to see her so afraid.

It seemed to Harrah that he knew the men also, an intuitive knowledge based on long experience.

"You smell of law," he said to them. He laughed. "You've forgotten where you are. This is Komar."

The large man shook his head. "We're not law. This is—personal."

"Let us have no trouble, Earthman," said the Martian. "We have no quarrel with you. It is only the girl-thing we want." He began to move closer to Harrah, slowly, like a man approaching a dangerous animal. At the same time the others moved in also.

"Unfasten your belt." said the large man to Harrah. "Let it drop."

"Don't let them take me." whispered Marith.

Harrah lowered his hands to his belt.

He moved then, very swiftly. But they were swift too and there were three of them. Harrah had not quite cleared his gun from the holster when the Martian's weapon took him club-fashion across the side of the head. He fell. He heard his gun clatter sharply against stone, far away where someone had kicked it. He heard Marith cry out.

With infinite effort he raised himself on his hands. Wavering bands of blackness and intense light obscured his vision. But he saw dimly that the Venusian had caught the girl and that the other two were struggling to subdue her, and that her struggle was beyond belief, the small white body fighting to be free.

He tried to rise and could not. In a minute they had borne her down, the three of them. The slender wrists were snared and bound.

One of the men produced a cloth that gleamed like metal and raised it above her head.

They seemed to recede from Harrah, gliding away down a street curiously lengthened into some dark dimension of pain. The echoes of their grunts and scufflings rang queerly muffled in his ears. But he saw, quite clearly, the last despairing look that Marith gave him before the shining cloth descended and hid her face.

His heart was wrenched with sorrow for her and a terrible rage rose in him against the men. He tried to get up and go after her and for a time he thought he had but when his sight cleared a little he realized that he had only crawled a few inches. How long the effort had taken him he did not know but the street was empty and there was no sound.

"Marith," he said. "Marith!"

Then he looked up, and saw that her brothers were standing over him, immensely tall, their beautiful strange faces very white in the shifting light of the moons.

III: A Broken Edge

One of the Wanderers reached down and gathered Harrah's shirtfront into his hand. Without effort, he lifted the Earthman to his feet. He looked into Harrah's face with eyes that were like Marith's, black and deep, charged with some cruel anger of the soul.

"Where is she?" he demanded. "Where have they taken her?"

"I don't know." Harrah found that he could stand up. He tried to shake off the Wanderer's grip. "Where did you come from? How did you—"

"Find her." The hand that would not be shaken off tightened on Harrah's shirt until the cloth was drawn close around his throat. "You took her away, Earthman. Between you and the dogs something has happened that was not meant to happen. You took her—now find her!"

Harrah said between his teeth, "Let go."

"Let him go, Kehlin," said one of the others. "He will be no use dead."

Almost reluctantly the throttling grip relaxed and was gone. Harrah stepped back. He was furious but he was also more than a little frightened. Again, as with Marith, he had touched something strange in this man Kehlin. The terrible relentless strength of that strangling hand seemed more than human.

Then he swayed and nearly fell and realized that he was still dizzy from the blow and probably not thinking very clearly.

The man called Kehlin said, with iron patience, "She must be found quickly. At once, do you understand? She is in great danger."

Harrah remembered his last sight of Marith's face. He remembered her fear and the quiet deadly urgency with which the three strangers had gone about the taking of her. He knew that Kehlin spoke the truth.

"I'll get Tok," said Harrah. "He can find out where she is."

"Who is Tok?"

Harrah explained. "The aboriginals know everything that goes on in Komar almost before it happens."

He turned, suddenly in a hurry to get on to his lodgings and look for Tok, but Kehlin said sharply, "Wait. I can do it more quickly."

Harrah stopped, a cold tingle sweeping across his skin. Kehlin's face had the same look that he had seen on Marith's before, the odd expression of one listening to distant voices. There was a moment of silence and then the Wanderer smiled and said, "Tok is coming."

One point of mystery cleared up for Harrah. "Telepaths. That's how you found me, how you knew what had happened to Marith. She was calling to you to hurry."

Kehlin nodded. "Unfortunately it's a limited talent. We can communicate among ourselves when we wish, and we have some control over minds of the lower orders, that are animal or very near it, like Tok's. But I cannot read or even trace the minds of the men who have taken my sister—and she is being prevented from using her own ability to talk to me."

"They put a cloth over her head," said Harrah. "A shining sort of cloth."

"Thought waves are electrical in nature," said Kehlin. "They can be screened."

After that no one spoke. They stood in the empty space under the blank walls of the houses and waited.

Presently among the shadows a darker shadow moved. Slowly, with a terrible reluctance, it came toward them into the moonlight and Harrah saw that it was Tok. Tok, creeping, cringing, bent as though under a heavy burden—not wanting to come but drawn as a fish is drawn unwilling by hook and line.

20

The hook and line of Kehlin's mind. Harrah glanced from the Wanderer's still face to the awful misery of fear in Tok's eyes and a wave of anger swept over him, mingled with a certain dread.

"Tok," he said gently. "Tok!"

The aboriginal turned his head and gave Harrah one look of hopeless pleading—just such a look as Marith had given when the strangers took her away. Then he crouched down at Kehlin's feet and stayed there, shivering.

Impulsively, Harrah started forward and one of Kehlin's brothers caught him by the arm.

"If you want to save her—be still!"

Harrah was still, and felt the aching of his flesh where the man had gripped it, as though with five clamps of steel instead of human fingers.

Kehlin did not speak and the only sound that came from Tok was a sort of unconscious whimpering. But after a minute or two Kehlin said, "He knows where she is. He will guide us."

*

Tok had already turned to go. The men followed him. Harrah saw that Tok's step was swift now, almost eager. But the terror had not left him.

Kehlin watched him and his eyes were black and deep as the spaces beyond the stars.

Demons. Demons with the eyes of darkness.

A shiver of superstitious fear went over Harrah. Then he looked again at the Wanderers in their tawdry rags—outcasts of an outcaste tribe, selling their sister's beauty in the marketplace for the sake of a few coins, and his awe left him.

He had caught too much of it from the aboriginals, who could make an evil spirit out of every shadow.

THE DANCING GIRL OF GANYMEDE

He began to think again of Marith, and the yellow-eyed Martian who had cracked his skull, and his knuckles itched.

He had no weapon now except a knife he carried under his shirt but he felt that he could make shift.

Abruptly he asked a question that had been on the top of his mind. "What did the men want with her?"

One of the Wanderers shrugged. "She is beautiful."

"That was not in their minds," said Harrah. "Nor is it yours."

"An old feud," said Kehlin harshly. "A blood feud."

Something about his voice made Harrah shiver all over again.

There was something strange about Komar now. After that brief violence of the dogs, nothing stirred. The sound of voices came from the roofless houses, a sort of uneasy muttering that burst into sharper cadence around the wine shops.

But no man walked in the streets. Even the dogs were gone.

Harrah was sure that eyes watched them from the darkness, as Marith and her captors had been watched. But it was only a feeling. The aboriginals themselves were intangible as smoke.

Tok led the way swiftly, doubling back toward the lower side of the bazaar. Here was a section that Harrah never visited—the Quarter of the Sellers of Dreams. Poetic name for a maze of filthy rat-runs stinking with the breath of nameless substances. The sliding roofs were always closed and what few voices could be heard were beyond human speech.

They came to a house that stood by itself at the end of an alley. It looked as though it had stood a long time by itself, the fecund weeds growing thick around the door, rooting in the chinks of the walls.

There was no light, no sound. But Tok stopped and pointed.

22

After a moment Kehlin nodded. With that gesture he dismissed Tok, forgot him utterly, and the aboriginal went with three loping strides into the shadows and was gone.

*

Kehlin moved forward, treading noiselessly in the dust.

The others followed. Around at the side was a wing, partially destroyed in some old quake. A thick stubby tree had sprouted in the dirt floor, its branches spreading out over the broken walls.

Without waiting for Kehlin's orders Harrah swung up into the tree and climbed from there to the coping of the house, where he could look down upon the roof.

The sliding sections were closed. But they were old and rotted and through the gaps Harrah saw a dim glow of light. Somewhere below a lantern burned and a man was talking.

The Wanderers were beside him now on the coping, moving with great care on the crumbling brick. Their eyes caught the lantern-glow with a feral glitter, giving them a look unutterably cruel and strange.

Harrah thought they had forgotten him now as completely as they had forgotten Tok.

He shifted position until he could see directly down through a hole in the roof. Kehlin was beside him, very close.

The man's voice came up to them, slow, deliberate, without pity.

"We've come a long way for this. We didn't have to. We could have stayed safe at home and let somebody else do the worrying. But we came. One man from each world—men, hear me? Human men."

His shadow fell broad and black across the floor, across Marith. A large shadow, ponderous, immovable. The girl lay on the floor. The metallic cloth still covered her head and a gag had been added outside it, to keep her from screaming. She was still bound but the cords had been replaced by metal cuffs, connected by wires that led

23

to a little black box. A tiny portable generator, Harrah thought, and was filled with fury.

"You're tough," said the man. "But we're tough too. And we won't go away empty handed. I'll ask you once more. How many—and where?"

Marith shook her head.

A lean dark hand that could only have belonged to the Martian reached out and pressed a stud on the black box. The body of the girl stiffened, was shaken with agony.

Harrah gathered himself. And in the instant before he jumped Kehlin moved so that his shoulder struck the Earthman a hard thrusting blow and sent him plunging head foremost through the roof.

There was a great splintering of rotten wood. The whole room was suddenly revealed to Harrah—the three men looking upward, the girl scarlet and white against the brown floor, the small black box, all rushing up, up to meet him.

He grasped at a broken edge of roof. It crumbled in his hands, and he saw the Venusian step back, it seemed very slowly, to get out of his way. The momentary breaking of his fall enabled Harrah to get his feet under him and he thought that he was not going to die at once, he would surely live long enough to break Kehlin's neck instead of his own.

He hit the floor in a shower of dust and splinters. Half smiling the Martian drew his gun.

IV: As Leopards...

After that for a moment no one moved. The dust of years sifted down on them. Another board fell with a crash. Harrah gasped for the breath that had been knocked out of him and the girl writhed in her uninterrupted pain. A brief moment of stillness in which the Earthman, the Martian and the Venusian stared at Harrah and thought of nothing else.

Then, very stealthily and swiftly, the Wanderers dropped through the open roof as leopards drop on their quarry from above. In a way, it was beautiful to watch—the marvelous grace and strength with which they moved, the flashing of the three bright silent blades. A ballet with knives. The Martian's gun went off once. It didn't hit anything. The big Earthman turned to grapple with Kehlin and grunted as the steel went home between his ribs.

Harrah got up. There didn't seem to be any place for him in that fight. It was over too fast, so fast that it seemed impossible that three men could die in so few seconds. The faces of Marith's brothers were cold with a terrible coldness that turned Harrah sick to look at them.

He stepped over the body of the Venusian, noting how the curling silver hair was mottled with crimson and dark dust. He cut the power from the black box and Marith relaxed slowly, her flesh still quivering. He tore the gag and the metal cloth from her head, and thought that men who could do this thing to a girl deserved to die. And yet he took no joy in it.

Marith looked up at him and he thought she smiled. He lifted her and held her in his arms, touching her with awkward gentle hands.

The big Earthman raised his head. Even death he would meet on his own time, refusing to be hurried. He saw what had been done, and there was something now in his broad stolid face that startled Harrah—a grim and shining faith.

He looked at the Wanderers with a look of bitter fury in which there was no acknowledgment of defeat.

"All right," he said. "All right. You're safe for a while now. You set a trap and you baited it with her and it worked—and you're safe now. But you can't hide. The very dogs know you. There's no place for you in earth, heaven or hell. If it takes every drop of human blood in the System to drown you we'll do it."

He turned to Harrah, kneeling in the dirt with Marith in his arms.

"Don't you know what they are?" he demanded. "Are you in love with that and you don't know what it is?"

Harrah felt Marith shudder and sigh against him and before he could speak Kehlin had stooped, smiling, over the big man. The Wanderer's knife made one quick dainty motion and there were no more words, only a strangled grunting such as a butchered pig makes when it falls. Then silence.

Marith's fingers tightened on Harrah's wrist. She tried to rise and he helped her up and steadied her.

Still smiling, Kehlin came across the room, the knife swinging languidly in his hand.

Marith said, "Wait."

Kehlin's smile turned into something sardonic. As one who is in no hurry he waited, coming only far enough so that the blood of the big Earthman would not touch his sandals.

Marith looked up into Harrah's face. There was no hatred in her eyes now.

"Is it true?" she asked. "Do you love me?"

Harrah could not answer. He looked at the dead men and the three silent beings that stood over them and there was a sickness in him, a sickness beyond the fear of death.

"What are you?" he said to them. "The dogs know you. Tok knows you. But I don't know you."

His gaze came back to Marith. She had not taken her eyes from him. They broke his heart.

"Yes," he said, with a queer harshness. "Yes, I guess I love you as much as you can make any meaning out of the word." The smell of blood lay heavy and sweet on the air and the blade gleamed in Kehlin's hand and it seemed a strange word to be speaking in this place. It had a jeering sound of laughter.

Marith whispered, "Kiss me."

*

Stiffly, slowly, Harrah bent and kissed her on the mouth. Her lips were cool and very sweet and a queer wild pang rang through him so that his flesh contracted as though from pain or fear and his heart began a great pounding.

He stepped back and said, "You're not human."

"No," she answered softly. "I am android." Presently she smiled. "I told you, Earthman. I am Marith. I am Forbidden."

She did not weep. She had no human tears. But her eyes were heavy with the sadness of all creation.

"From time to time," she murmured, "men and women have loved us. It is a great sin and they are punished for it and we are destroyed. We have no souls and are less than the dogs that tear at us. Ashes to ashes, dust to dust—even that is denied us for we are not born of the earth, of Adam's clay. The hand of man made us, not the hand of God, and it is true that we have no place in heaven or hell."

"We will make a place," said Kehlin, and his fingers played with the shining knife. There was no sadness about him. He looked at the dead men, the man of Earth, the man of Venus, the man of Mars.

THE DANCING GIRL OF GANYMEDE

"On their worlds we will make a place. Heaven has no meaning for us nor hell. Only the life we have now, the life man gave us. You, Earthman! How long have you been out here beyond the Belt?"

"A long time," said Harrah. "A long, long time."

"Then you haven't heard of the war." Kehlin's white teeth glittered. "The secret quiet war against us—the slaves, the pets, the big wonderful toys that grew so strong we frightened the men who made us. It's not strange you haven't heard. The governments tried to keep it secret. They didn't want a panic, people killing each other in mistake for runaway androids. We were so hard to detect, you see, once we shed our uniforms and got rid of our tattoo marks." He stirred the Martian with his foot, the dark face turned upward, snarling even in death.

"It took men like this to recognize us," he said. "Men trained in the laboratories before they were trained against crime. We thought we were safe here, far beyond the law, but we had to be sure. Law wouldn't matter if word got back to the Inner Worlds. They would come out and destroy us." He laughed. "Now we're sure."

"For a time," said Marith. "There will be others like them."

"Time," said Kehlin. "A little time. That's all we need."

He moved again toward Harrah, casually swift, as though one more thing needed to be done.

Harrah watched him come. He did not quite believe, even now. He was remembering androids as he had known of them long ago—Kehlin had named them. The slaves, the pets, the big wonderful toys. Synthetic creatures built of chemical protoplasm, molded in pressure tanks, sparked to intelligent life by the magic of cosmic rays drawn pure from outer space.

Creatures made originally to do the work that human flesh was too frail for—the dangerous things, the experiments with pressure and

28

radiation, the gathering of data from places where men could not go, the long lonely grinding jobs that tear human nerves to pieces.

For man had built better than Nature. The androids were not hampered by the need of food, air and water. A few ounces of chemicals every year or so kept them going. Their lungs were ornamental, for the purpose of speech only. They had no complicated internal structure to break down and their flesh was tough-celled, all but indestructible.

And because they could be made beautiful, because they had strength and grace and endurance beyond the human, their uses had widened. Entertainers, household servants, fashionable adjuncts to expensive living. Things. Objects to be bought and sold like machines. And they had not been content.

Kehlin's eyes were brilliant with the glory of hate. He was as splendid and inevitable as the angel of death and, looking at him, Harrah became aware of a bitter truth—the truth that the big Earthman had denied with his dying breath. Man had wrought too well. These were the natural inheritors of the universe.

Marith said again, "Wait."

This time Kehlin did not stop.

Marith faced him, standing between him and Harrah's vulnerable body.

"I have earned this right," she said. "I demand it."

Kehlin answered without a flicker of emotion. "This man must die." And he would not stop.

Marith would not move and behind her back Harrah drew his own knife into his hand. Futile as it was he could not submit to butchery without at least the gesture of fighting back. He looked into Kehlin's face and shuddered, an inward shudder of the soul.

*

Marith spoke.

"This man has already helped us greatly—perhaps he has saved us by saving me." She pointed to the bodies. "We're not free of their kind and what we have to do can't be done in a minute. We need supplies from Komar—metals, tools, chemicals, many things. If we get them ourselves we run the risk of being recognized. But if we had an agent, a go-between—" She paused, then added, "A human."

Kehlin had at last halted to listen. One of the other men—Harrah could not, somehow, stop thinking of them as men—spoke up.

"That is worth thinking about, Kehlin. We can't spend all our time in the public squares, watching for spies."

Kehlin looked across Marith's white shoulder at the Earthman, and shook his head.

"Trust a human?" He laughed.

"There are ways to prevent betrayal," said Marith. "Ways you know of."

And the android who had spoken before echoed, "That is so."

Kehlin played with the knife and continued to watch Harrah but he did not move. Harrah said hoarsely, "To the devil with you all. No one has asked me whether I'm willing to betray my own kind."

Kehlin shrugged. "You can join them quite easily." he said, and glanced at the bodies. Marith turned and took Harrah by the arms. Her touch sent that queer pang through his flesh again, and it was strangely sweet.

"Death is yours for the asking, now or later. But think, Earthman. Perhaps there is justice on our side too. Wait a little before you die."

She had not changed, he thought. Her little white feet that had walked beside his in the dust of Komar, her voice that had spoken to him through the moonlight—they had not changed. Only her eyes were different.

30

Marith's eyes and himself, because of what he knew. And yet he remembered.

He did not know what he held—child, woman or some alien wicked creature, close in the hollow of his arm. But she was very lovely and he would not let her go.

He drew a long breath. Her eyes, searching his, were a beauty and a pain so poignant that he could neither bear it nor look away.

"All right." he said. "I'll wait."

V: The Same Beauty

They had come a long way down from the plateau of Komar, into the jungle that laps around it like a hungry ocherous sea. They had come by steep and secret ways that were possible only to an aboriginal—or an android.

Harrah, who had been handed bodily down the dizzy cliffs, was more conscious than ever of his human inferiority. He was exhausted, his bones ached with wrenching, and his nerves were screaming. But Marith, so small and sweetly made, had dropped over the precipices like a little white bird, unaided, and she was quite unwearied.

Once during the descent Kehlin had paused, holding Harrah without effort over a thousand feet of sheer space, between the wheeling moons and the darkness.

He had smiled, and said, "Tok is following. He is afraid but he is following you."

Harrah himself was too much afraid even to be touched.

Now they stood, the four androids and the man from Earth, in the jungle of Ganymede. Vapor from some hidden boiling spring drifted through the tangle of branches and flowering vines, the choking wanton growth of a hothouse run wild. There was a taste of sulphur in the air and a smell of decay and a terrible heat.

Kehlin seemed to be listening to something. He turned slightly once, then again as though getting his direction. Then he started off with complete certainty and the others followed. No one spoke. No one had told Harrah where they were going or why.

Only Marith kept close to him and now and again he would meet her gaze and she would smile, a smile wistful and sad as far-off music. And Harrah hated her because he was weary and drenched with sweat and every step was a pain.

33

THE DANCING GIRL OF GANYMEDE

He hoped that Tok was still following them. It was comforting to think of that furry shape gliding noiselessly along, at home in the jungle, part of it. Tok was not human either. But he too could feel pain and weariness and fear. He and Harrah were brothers in blood.

The sky was blotted out. The eternal moonlight sifted through the trees, restless, many-hued, tinged here and there with blood from the red glow of Jupiter. The forest was very still. It seemed as endless as the dark reaches of the dreams that come with fever, and Harrah fancied that it held its breath and waited.

Once they came to a place where the trees were slashed by a vast sickle of volcanic slag. To the north a gaunt cone stood up against the sky, crooked, evil, wearing a plume of smoke on its brow. The smell of sulphur was very strong and heat breathed out of the mountain's flanks with a hissing sound like the laughter of serpents.

Lightly, swiftly, the white-skinned beautiful creatures sped across that blasted plain and the man came staggering after them.

Three times they passed through rude villages. But the huts were empty. Word had gone through the jungle as though the wind carried it and the aboriginals had vanished.

Kehlin smiled. "They have hidden their women and children," he said, "but the men watch us. They crouch in the trees around our camp. They are afraid and they watch."

At length through the stillness Harrah began to hear a sound very strange in this primal forest—the clangor of forges. Then, quite suddenly, they came to the edge of a place where the undergrowth had been cleared away and their journey was over.

The picked bones of a rusty hull lay among the trees and beneath its skeletal shadow there was motion. Long sheds had been built. Lights burned in them and figures passed to and fro and vast heaps of metal torn from the ship lay ready to be worked.

34

Kehlin said softly, "Look at them, Earthman. Thirty-four, counting ourselves. All that are left. But the finest, the best. The lords of the world."

Harrah looked. Men, a few women or creatures made in their semblance, all stamped with the same beauty, the same tireless strength. There was something wonderful about them, working, building, untouched by their environment, apart from it, using it only as a tool to serve them. Something wonderful, Harrah thought, struggling for breath in the bitter heat. Wonderful and frightening.

Kehlin had apparently given them the whole story telepathically, for they did not pause from their work to ask questions. Only they glanced at Harrah as he passed and in their eyes he saw the shadow of fate. Kehlin said, "We will go into the ship."

*

Some of the inner cabins were still intact. The ship had been old and very small. Stolen, Harrah guessed, the best that they could do, but they had made it good enough. No more than ten men could have survived in its cramped quarters. Yet thirty-four androids had ridden it across deep space. Darkness, lack of air and food, did not bother them.

"We brought what equipment we could." said Kehlin. "The rest we must fashion for ourselves." The sound of the forges echoed his words. He led Harrah into what had been the captain's cabin. It was crammed with delicate electronic apparatus, some of which Harrah recognized as having to do with encephalographs and the intricacies of thought-waves.

There was no room for furniture. Kehlin indicated a small clear space on the deck-plates. "Sit down."

Harrah did not obey at once and the android smiled. "I'm not going to torture you and if I had wished to kill you I could have done so long ago. We must have complete understanding, you and I." He paused and Harrah was perfectly aware of the threat behind his words. "Our minds must speak, for that is the only way to understanding."

Marith said softly, "That is so, Earthman. Don't be afraid."

Harrah studied her. "Will I be able to understand you then?"

"Perhaps."

Harrah sat down on the hard iron plates and folded his hands between his knees to hide their trembling. Kehlin worked smoothly for a time. Harrah noted the infinite deftness of his movements. A distant humming rose in the cabin and was lost to hearing. Kehlin placed round electrodes at the Earthman's temples and Harrah felt a faint tingling warmth.

Then the android knelt and looked into his eyes and he forgot everything, even Marith, in the depths of that passionate alien gaze.

"Seventy-three years ago I was made." said Kehlin. "How long have you lived, Earthman? Thirty years? Forty? How much have you done, what have you learned? How is the strength of your body? How is the power of your mind? What are your memories, your hopes? We will exchange these things, you and I—and then we will know each other."

A deep tremor shook Harrah. He did not speak. Two sharp movements of Kehlin's hands. The cabin darkened around him. A swift reeling vertigo, an awful plunging across some unknown void, a loss of identity...

Harrah cried out in deadly fear and the voice was not his own.

He could not move. Vague images crowded his mind, whirling, trampling, unutterably strange.

Memories coming back, confused, chaotic, a painful meshing of realities. Silence. Darkness. Peace.

He lay at rest. It seemed that there had never been anything but this bodiless negation in the very womb of sleep. He had no memories. He had no identity. He was nothing. He was without thought or trouble, wrapped in the complete peacefulness of not-being. Forever and forever, the timeless sleep.

Then, from somewhere out of the void, vast and inescapable as the stroke of creation upon nothingness, a command came. The command to wake.

He awoke.

Like a comet, cruel and bright across the slumbrous dark, awareness came. A sudden explosion of being, leaping full upon him with a blaze and a shriek. Here was no slow gentle realization, softened by the long years of childhood. Here was inundation, agony—self.

The little part of Harrah that remained cringed before that terrible awakening. No human brain could have borne it. Yet it was as though the memory were his own. He felt the flood tide of life roar in and fill his emptiness, felt the fabric of his being shudder, withstand and find itself.

He knew that he was remembering the moment of Kehlin's birth. He opened his eyes.

Vision keen as an eagle's, careless of darkness, of shadows, of blinding light. He saw a tall Earthman with a haggard face, who sat before him on the rusty deck and regarded him with strange eyes. An Earthman named Tony Harrah. Himself. Yet it was Kehlin the android who looked out of his eyes.

He started up, wavering on the brink of madness, and Marith's hands were on his shoulders, holding him steady.

"Don't be afraid. I am here."

It was not her voice speaking to him but her mind. He could hear it now. He could feel it touching his, sweet and full of comfort. Quite suddenly he realized that she was no longer a stranger. He knew her now. She was—Marith.

Her mind spoke gently. "Remember, Earthman. Remember the days of Kehlin." He remembered.

VI: Lords of the World

He remembered the laboratory, the birthplace, the doorway to the world of men. He remembered the moment when he first rose up from the slab where he had lain and stood before his makers, embodied and alive. He remembered the fine smooth power of his limbs, the bright newness of sounds, the wonderful awareness of intellect.

Brief vivid flashes, the highlights of seventy-three years of existence, coming to Harrah as though they were his own. The long intensive training—*Kehlin, Type A, technical expert*. The ease of learning, the memory that never faltered, the growth of mental power until it overtopped the best of the human teachers.

He remembered the moment when Kehlin first looked upon the redness of human blood and realized how frail were the bodies of men.

He watched the gradual development of emotion.

Emotion is instinctive in natural life. In the android, Harrah saw it grow slowly from the intellect. An odd sort of growth, like a tree of crystal with clear, sharp branches—but alive and no less powerful than the blind sprawling impulses of man. Different, though. Very different

One great root was lacking—the root of lust. Kehlin's hungers were not of the flesh and because he was free of this he was free also of greed and cruelty and—this came to Harrah with a shock of surprise—of hate.

In this uncanny sharing of another mind he remembered testing experimental ships at velocities too great for human endurance. He had enjoyed that, hurtling across infinity like a rogue asteroid with a silent shriek of speed.

THE DANCING GIRL OF GANYMEDE

He remembered being cast adrift in space alone. He wore no protective armor. The cold could not harm him and he had no need of air. He looked at the naked blaze of the universe and was not awed. The magnificence of space did not crush him with any sense of his own smallnesss.

He did not expect to be as big as a star. Rather, for the first time, he felt free. Free of the little worlds, the little works of men. They were bound but he was not. Distance and time were no barriers to him. He was brother to the roving stars because both had been made, not born. He wanted to go out to them.

The rescue ship came and took him in but he never forgot his dream of the other suns and his longing to go among them, clear out to the edge of the universe.

Instead he gathered data for the scientists in the forbidden places of the Solar System. He walked the chasms of Mercury's Darkside, where the human mind will crack in the terrible night, where the black mountain ranges claw at the stars and no life has ever been or ever will be. He went deep into the caverns of the Moon. He went into the Asteroid Belt and charted a hundred deadly little worlds alone while his masters waited safely in the shelter of their ship.

And still he was outcaste—a thing, an android. Men used him and ignored him. They were human and he was an object out of nature, vaguely repulsive, a little frightening. He had not eyen any contact with his own kind. As though they had some foreknowledge of trouble men kept their androids apart. Harrah was aware, in Kehlin's mind, of a piercing loneliness.

There's no place for you in earth, heaven or hell!

Marith's thought crossed his like the falling of tears. "For us there was no comfort, no hope, no refuge. We were made in your image, man and woman. Yet you were cruel gods for you made a lie and gave us the intelligence to know it. You denied us even dignity. And—we did not ask to be made."

Kehlin said, "It is enough."

Once again Harrah was flung across a reeling darkness. This time the change was not so frightening but in a way it was worse. He did not realize that until he was again fully aware of himself. Then he was conscious of a bitter contrast, a thing both saddening and shameful.

The mind of the android, that he had shared for that brief time, had been as a wide space flooded with light. His own seemed cluttered and dark to him now, haunted by ugly shapes that crept along the borders of consciousness. All the splendid strength was gone. The crushing weariness of his body descended upon him, and he looked down almost with disgust at his unsteady hands.

He did not ask what Kehlin had found in him. He did not want to know.

"Can you understand now how we felt?" asked Kehlin. "Can you understand how we learned to hate men?"

Harrah shook his head. "You don't hate." he said. "You don't know the meaning of hate as we do. What I mistook for hatred in you was something much bigger. I'd call it pride."

He had seen so much in Kehlin's mind. Pity for man in his weakness, admiration for his courage because he had survived and built in spite of his weakness. Perhaps even gratitude.

*

But Kehlin had called his fellow androids the lords of the world, and he was right. They were proud and their pride was just and they would not live in chains.

Kehlin shrugged. "Call it what you will, it doesn't matter." He looked at Harrah, and for the first time the Earthman saw in the android a softening, almost a weariness.

THE DANCING GIRL OF GANYMEDE

"It isn't that we want to rule men. It isn't that we want power! It's only that men have driven us through fear. Should we go down into nothingness because men fear us? Remember, we don't even have the hope of a hereafter to soften our going!"

He shook his head. "It will be a long fight and a bitter one. I don't want it, none of us do. But we must survive and to do that we must rule and perhaps men will come out the better for it. There will never be any peace or real advancement until these wretched little worlds are governed by those who are not of the mass but above it, not driven by every wind that blows."

He was silent a moment, brooding, and then he echoed Marith's words.

"Fear. Always fear. The human race is ridden with it. Lust and fear and greed and sorrow. If only they had not been afraid of us!"

The old blaze of anger came again into his eyes. "With acid and with fire they destroyed us, Earthman. Thirty-four, all that are left. But not for long. Human reproduction is slow and clumsy, but not ours. Only a little time and there will be more of us, many more, and we will go back and take what is ours."

He said it very quietly and Harrah heard truth in his voice like the tolling of a bell—the passing-bell for the mastery of human kind.

"Will you help us, Earthman, or will you die?"

Harrah did not answer and Marith said, "Let him rest."

Kehlin nodded. He left and Harrah was hardly aware of his going. The girl spoke to him gently and he rose and stumbled after her, out of the ship.

She led him to a space apart from the main sheds, an unfinished lean-to where only a dim light filtered from the work-lamps. It was dark under the trees and hot. Terribly hot. Harrah sat down on the moist ground and put his head between his hands and there was still no answer in him, only a great blankness.

Marith waited and did not speak.

After awhile Harrah lifted his head and looked at her. "Why did you save me from Kehlin's knife?"

She answered slowly, "I'm not like Kehlin. I was made only for beauty, a dancer. My mind won't reach so high. It asks questions but they're little ones, of small account."

"What questions, Marith?"

"I have been alive for nineteen years. My owner was very proud of me and I made him a great deal of money. And everywhere I went, in every city, on every world, I watched men and women. I saw the way they looked at each other, the way they smiled. Many of the women were not beautiful or talented. But men loved them and they were happy."

Harrah remembered her words—I hate all men and women also. *Especially women.*

"When I was through working." she said, "my owner put me away like a dancing doll until it was time to work again. I had nothing to do but sit alone and think and wonder."

She was close to Harrah. Her face was indistinct in the gloom, a shadowy thing of dreams.

"When you thought that I was human you said you loved me. I think that is why I saved you from the knife."

There was a long silence and then Harrah said the words she was waiting for, wanting to hear, and they were the truth.

"I love you now."

She said, very softly, "But not as you would love a woman."

He remembered her dancing in the bazaar, the ancient sensual dance that became in her a thing of sheer loveliness.

43

"No," he said. "But that's because you're more than human, not less."

He took her into his arms and he knew now what he held there. Not child nor woman nor any wicked thing but a creature innocent and beautiful as the moonlight and as far beyond him.

He held her close and it was as though for a moment he held his own youth again, the short bright days before he had learned the things Kehlin had named—lust and fear and greed and sorrow. He held her close and there was no passion in him, only an immense tenderness, a longing and regret so deep that his heart was near to breaking. He had his answer.

*

Marith drew away from him and rose, turning her face into the darkness so that he could not see her eyes. She said, "I should have let you die in Komar. It would have been easier then for both of us."

An eerie chill ran over Harrah. "You can read my mind now." He got up, very slowly.

She nodded. "Kehlin more than I because he shared it fully. That was what I meant when I reminded him that there were ways to prevent betrayal. If I were human I would tell you to run quickly and hide yourself from Kehlin and I would hope. But I am not human and I know there is no hope."

She turned toward him then, clear in the barred moonlight.

"Like to like." she whispered. "You have your burden and your pride and you would not be free of either. Kehlin was right. And yet I wish—oh, I wish."

Quite suddenly she was gone and Harrah was reaching out his hand to emptiness.

For a long moment he did not move. He heard the sound of movement in the camp and knew that the telepathic warning had gone out and that within a few seconds he would be dead but he could only think that Marith was gone and he had lost her.

Then from the dark jungle, swift with love and terror, Tok came crying out to his lord.

Harrah had forgotten Tok, who had followed him down from the safety of Komar. He had forgotten a number of things. Now he remembered. He remembered Kehlin's words and the three men who had died in Komar and why they had died.

He remembered that he was human and could hope where there was no hope. "Come, Lord! Run!"

Harrah ran. And it was already too late.

The androids came, the fleet lithe creatures heading him off. Tok stood not thirty feet away, but he knew that he could never make it.

He stopped running. He saw Kehlin among those who came to trap him and he saw the gun the android carried now in place of the knife.

With acid and with fire they destroyed us...

With fire.

It was Harrah's turn to cry out to Tok, to the unseen watchers in the trees. He shouted with all his strength in the split second before he fell and his words carried over even the sound of the shot.

He thought that Tok was gone. He thought that there was an answer from the jungle but he was not sure. He was not sure of anything but pain.

*

He lay where he had fallen and he knew that he would continue to lie there because his leg was broken above the knee. He looked incuriously at the dark blood seeping around the wound, and then up into the face of Kehlin, wondering why the android had aimed so low.

45

Reading his thought Kehlin answered, "You had already spoken. And—I preferred you should die with us."

For a long time after that he did not speak and there was a great silence on the clearing. The androids stood, the thirty-four tall splendid beings who were the last of their kind, and they made no sound.

The jungle also was very still. But the aboriginals had done their work well and already there was a taint of smoke on the air and the wind blew hot. The naked bones of the ship mocked them with the shelter they might have had. There was no refuge, no escape, and they knew it.

Harrah saw how Kehlin looked up at the sky, at the distant suns that light the edges of the universe. The jungle sighed and flames stood up among the trees all around them like a ring of spears. Harrah thought that humans were not alone in their knowledge of sorrow. Kehlin turned abruptly and called, "Marith!"

She came out from among the others and stood before him.

"Are you happy, Marith? You have done a human thing. You have behaved like a woman, wrecking empires for love."

He flung her down beside Harrah and then he shook his head slowly and said, "No, the blame is mine. I was the leader. I should have killed the man."

He laughed suddenly. "And so this is the end—and it does not come to us from the hands of man but from the paws of apes who have learned no more than the making of fire!"

Harrah nodded. "Apes," he said. "Yes. That's the gulf between us. That's why we fear you. You were never an ape."

He watched the ring of fire brighten and draw in. The pain in his leg was very great and he was bleeding and his mind seemed distant from his body and full of profound thoughts.

"We distrust anyone who is different," he said. "We always destroy them, one way or another."

He looked up at Kehlin. "Apes. A restless, unruly bunch, driven by passions and hungers you could never understand. You would not have been able to rule us. No one ever has. We can't even ourselves. So in the end you would have destroyed us."

Kehlin's eyes met his, the black, deep eyes, brilliant now with some terrible emotion that Harrah could not read.

"Perhaps," he said softly. "Perhaps. And you're proud, aren't you? The weakling has pulled down his betters and it makes him feel strong. You're proud to die because you think you've put an end to us. But you have not, Earthman! You have not!"

Standing very tall beneath the banners of red light that shook from the flaring trees Kehlin cried out strongly, shouting to the stars, to all creation.

"You made us once, you little men who love to feel like gods! You will make us again. You can't keep from it—and we will inherit the universe!"

Harrah knew now what was in Kehlin's mind. It was faith. He saw it in the faces of all those who stood with Kehlin, the beautiful creatures trapped and waiting under the crimson pall.

A great curtain of flame and falling ash swept between them, hiding the androids from Harrah's sight. A bitter pang struck through him, a wild regret, and he tried to call out, to say that he was sorry. But the words would not come and he felt ashamed and very small and full of a black and evil guilt. He bowed his head and wept.

*

Marith's voice spoke close beside him. "They are gone and soon we will be too and it is better so."

THE DANCING GIRL OF GANYMEDE

Harrah turned. He was amazed to see that there was a strange look of joy about her as though she had been released from some dark prison.

"Do you love me, Marith? Do you love me still after what I've done?"

She answered, "You have set me free."

He took her in his arms and held her and it came to him that only this way, only now, could they two have been joined. And he was happy.

www.ingramcontent.com/pod-product-compliance
Lightning Source LLC
Chambersburg PA
CBHW050908120626
46554CB00003B/1079